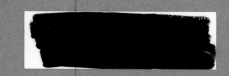

My Name Is *Not* Gussie

written and illustrated by **MIKKI MACHLIN**

HOUGHTON MIFFLIN COMPANY BOSTON 1999

Walter Lorraine Books

With Love: For Sammy (Golda Shmukler-Steinman) and all my other honeys.

Walter Lorraine Books

Copyright © 1999 by Mikki Machlin

Library of Congress Cataloging-in-Publication Data

Machlin, Mikki.
    My name is not Gussie / by Mikki Machlin.
        p.   cm.
    Summary: A young girl describes the difficulties and joys that she
and her family experience when they come from Russia to settle in
New York City in the early twentieth century. Based on stories from
the author's mother.
    ISBN 0-395-95646-3
    [1. Immigrants—Fiction.   2. Russian Americans—Fiction.   3. Jews—
United States—Fiction.   4. New York (N.Y.)—Fiction.]   I. Title.
PZ7.M4786285Mn   1999
[Fic]—dc21   99-19160
                                                                        CIP

Printed in the United States of America

WOZ   10 9 8 7 6 5 4 3 2 1

*When Mama scrubbed my face or fed me oatmeal, she told stories.
So not only my two children, five grandchildren, innumerable nieces
and nephews, but everybody else's could enjoy them, I wrote them down.
Here they are! The adventures of a little immigrant girl,
one hundred years ago.*

MIKKI MACHLIN

What an Adventure

Closer, slowly, steadily the cart crept closer until it filled my eyes, the whole front yard, and stopped. Hooray!

Bubba whispered, "Take, *ketzalah*—for you I baked a special *pletzle*."

Yum. I popped that cookie into my mouth. What? Me, who could always eat, suddenly couldn't swallow?

I stared at Bubba, my grandma, and Zaida, my grandpa. They always smiled at me. Why did they weep today? What did I do? I hugged them hard. But still they wept.

Now everybody was busy lugging, hugging, packing, and crying. All the grownups were crying. Only Louie and I ran around thrilled and delighted to be going . . . to America, the Golden Land. Who knew Bubba and Zaida weren't coming too? Everyone knew but us, the little ones. We crowded the cart. There were no seats for Bubba, for Zaida. Surely they will follow, I thought.

The cart bumped us through dark forests, past fields of golden grain until for the first time I saw a town. Streets crisscrossing every which way. Tall houses, short houses, so many houses—who could count? In my shtetl (or as you say, village), I knew every person, tree, cow, mule, and horse, and they knew me! Such sights! I wouldn't close an eye.

The cart left us. Now a new marvel. A train station. Hustle bustle, strangers everywhere. My brothers Sammy and Louie, Mama, carrying baby Mollie, Uncle Itzhak, Tante Feindele (my aunt), and cousin Heike clutched bags, bundles, and baskets, careful not to lose our few precious possessions. Tears jumped

suddenly, blurring my eyes. Something was missing. I'd lost something important. My Bubba, my Zaida, were far, far behind. They were nowhere in the crowd of people.

So many people all going together with us on a train. A train? Mama told me it was big, but this chain of long skinny houses on wheels stretched farther than my shtetl's street, clanged louder than the village church bells, was smokier than a hundred chimneys, and blacker than a starless sky. Could it eat us alive? Maybe not, because everybody rushed to squeeze in! Cousin Heike hid behind her hands so Tante dragged her up the train's steps, pushed through the crowd, and spread herself over three seats, pulling Heike down beside her. There they sat like gravestones. Uncle Itzie took turns with Mama sitting and holding baby Mollie. Sammy, Louie, and I sprawled over our pots, pans, pillows, and blankets that were piled between the seats. Our baggage spilled over, mixing with other people's belongings. What a mess!

We went swaying, rocking, rolling, belching all the way from Russia to the sea. Noise, smells, speed—everything I loved. Only Mama cried. So I wiped her tears. Her mama and papa, my Bubba and Zaida, were so far away already; all the places we knew were disappearing. Oy! I cried too. Now I understood.

"*Maidella*, my Golda." Mama hugged me. "Sha, sha, it's going to be wonderful, you'll see." She pretended, "I'm only upset because I can't find my *shissel* or my samovar. It's nothing!"

Someone had taken her precious bag of pots. I hope by mistake.

How Could You Eat?

What joy! Up the gangplank, onto the steamship we marched. Then rich people walked straight ahead, but we climbed down, down, down. The crowd pushed us forward. We couldn't stop. Too many people went with us, down the ladder, down under the decks of the great ship.

Whistles went *woooo-woooo!* We were off! Swaying into the great Atlantic Ocean.

People's eyes grew round.

Faces turned green.

Seasickness struck. People covered their mouths, staggering to the deck or lying like the dead. Poor Mama, poor uncle, poor Sammy. I almost felt sorry for the *kvetch* Queen Tante and Princess Heike. (Bossy Tante moaned if things were bad. So? Okay. She also moaned when things were good! For no reason Heike also knew how to groan. Who could believe them? On this occasion I made an exception.)

Louie and I ran to the deck. But not to throw up. No—we watched the waves, thrilled. The ship went so fast we imagined we were flying. Flying to the Golden Land. Flying to America. We could also eat. Every day. You think this is not unusual? You never lived in a sour, smelly, dim, rocking, rolling, rat-infested darkness called steerage for three weeks. Most people were seasick, yuck! Was there water to wash in? Ha! So who could eat? Louie and I could. We held our noses, pulled goodies out of the big basket of food Bubba had packed, ran to the deck, and played restaurant. If a person looked hungry, we asked, "What would you like for supper tonight?"

"Borsht with liver knish and a bowl of farfel, please," some soul might answer.

"Here you are sir. Enjoy!"

We'd present maybe a piece of salami, a prune, a pickle.

"Delicious. My compliments to the chef," they'd say, nibbling delicately.

We would bow politely. Louie and I loved to share, and people appreciated the food. It made such a nice change from the hard tack, potatoes, and gruel fed to us in steerage.

A big ship is a dangerous place. How come two little children were running, doing whatever they pleased? Where was the mama? Poor, sweet Mama lay like a stone with a lemon on her nose, all day, all night, clutching baby Molly and trying not to breathe. A lemon? On her nose? Right, wise guy. What would you rather smell? Steerage stink or the faint, tangy fragrance of a dried-up citrus fruit?

Haircuts

Poor seasick Mama hardly knew where she was, let alone where we were, her wild kids, Louie and me. We loved that wild sea. The ship was our playground. Signs said Running On Deck Forbidden, but who could read? So I chased Louie, and Louie chased me.

"Gotcha," Louie yelled.

"Naa, naa, you can't catch me!" I shouted, ducking and turning just as a giant wave rammed the ship, tossing me in the air. Wham! I came down, spinning along the slippery deck toward the few ropes that protected steerage passengers from the angry, bottomless ocean. *Gott in Himmel,* the ropes were passing over my head! "Help! Heeelp!" I screamed. Screeching wind, roaring waves, drowned my voice. Doomed, I prayed.

"Not so fast, Golda. You can't get away so easy!" Louie pounced on my foot. "Tee hee! You're it now," he said, laughing, but Louie started to slide! We were dead. I knew it. Louie clung to my foot. He grabbed the rope. We hollered. Louie's hand was slipping. It was too hard to hold on. We gave up. We closed our eyes.

A big hand suddenly jerked our jackets. A voice boomed, "*Kindele!* What kind of game is this?"

So that's how we made a friend. His name was Yankel Moishe. His last name I forgot.

Yankel Moishe was always laughing. When he became sadder and sadder, Louie and I worried.

"What's wrong?" we asked.

"*Kinder,* I have no money for a ticket to Cleveland, where a job waits for me."

The closer we came to New York, the worse Yankel Moishe looked. He looked so terrible that I told him, "Yankel Moishe, the Statue of Liberty should see you smiling. I, myself, am going to comb my hair and look my very best for her."

Suddenly, out of nowhere, Moishe grinned. "Golda, you got it!"

Magic! What did I say? I wondered.

"*Kinder,* find for me a pair of scissors, a comb, a bowl, a pen and paper."

What for? I wondered some more. Still, Louie and I found everything.

Meanwhile, Yankel Moishe went around the deck declaiming loudly to all the gentlemen in steerage. "To get into the U.S.A. you need a Yankee-style hairdo. What? You never heard of such a thing? It's a big secret. Lucky for you I know all about it. For a little change I can fix you perfect."

Yankel Moishe was so honest-looking that men lined up for a special haircut. Yankel Moishe made money! Enough to go to Cleveland.

My Name Is Not Gussie

Everyone calls me Gussie now, but that's not my real name. My real name is Golda. Golda turned into Augusta, Gussie for short. How did it happen that Golda became Augusta? Be patient! Here's how.

Cheering people, all dressed up, ran down the gangplank onto Ellis Island. Officials boomed, "Welcome! Line up. Forward, march!"

Eagerly we marched—where? Surprise! Straight into delousing showers—clothes and all. Stinky stuff soaked us, killing all our European bugs. Americans didn't need more lice. They had plenty already, thank you very much. Clothes stank, shrank, and wrinkled. Phew-ee! Were we smelly—but happy! Ellis Island was, after all, almost America.

Next came again lines. Doctors examined everyone. God forbid anything was wrong. Oy vey! On you they made "the chalk mark," meaning go back quick to Europe. We passed, waited for days, maybe weeks, till that last line—the final exam. Then uniformed inspectors looked carefully into our eyes and down our throats. To sick folk they said, "Go left, please," which meant stay in quarantine until you die or get well. Healthy people, they asked, "Name, please?"

One inspector liked names—not yours, the names in his head. He decreed on Friday, from 2 to 3 P.M., everybody will be Burkes! From 7 to 9 A.M., shazam! You're Lockwoods forevermore. He had power; he loved his job. Sometimes he invented new names, like Thurhhopper, or turned European names into English. Poof!

Mr. Stein is Mr. Stone. Guess whose line we picked? So who knew? They all looked alike, those tall Americans in uniform.

"Name?" he asked Tante, who was, of course, first in line.

"Feindele Schmukler," she answered.

"Um, Schmukler means jeweler, right? You'll be Mrs. Jewel here," he declared.

Tante took a very deep breath, puffed up, and turned purple, proclaiming, "Mistuh, my brother-in-law is already American. Name? Schmukler. One family, one name. We are not now and never will be Jewels!"

"A Jewel you ain't," he retorted, glaring at tubby Tante, then winked. "So, welcome, Fanny Schmukler."

Did Tante win? Heike, Sammy, Louie—they passed and kept their names.

"Next," said the inspector.

"Golda Schmukler is my name." I grinned up as the tall man bent over me. "Golda's no name—naa. A little girl needs a big name, so you'll always remember landing in the U.S.A. Oho!" He laughed. "Lucky you it ain't winter, you would be February Schmukler. It's summer, so, hello, Augusta!"

Another man wrote on my tag, "Augusta Schmukler to N.Y."

"Welcome to America," he said.

I was so astounded by becoming Augusta that I didn't see Mama and baby Molly turn left until Mama whispered, "Be good, my Goldala, I promise we'll be with you soon."

Our baby Molly was sick. When would I ever see them again?

Millionaires

Such cheers, such excitement, you wouldn't believe. The gangplank was down. We were, at last, really in the U.S.A.!

Uncle Itzhak waved to Papa waiting on the dock. Papa ran to us. He opened his arms; we jumped right in. He hugged and kissed us. Then he said, "Wooah! These are my *kinder?* Itzhak, you're sure?"

Papa held me high above his head. "This is my *maidella?* Golda? You came to my knee, now look! Such a young lady? Nah. And Louie and Sammy. Big, strong boys. Men! In sixteen months miracles happened!"

We felt so safe, so happy to be with our Papa again. It was our miracle.

He missed Mama and Molly. He worried. "What will be their fate?" But he hid his sorrow. He held us close and whispered, "Soon, soon, Mama and Molly will be with us—before you know it. You'll see. Come, come, kinder, to your new home."

So I rode on a trolley for the very first time. What a relief! The whole ride I never saw even once cops shooting robbers or cowboys on horses fighting Indians. Why should I expect such goings-on? In Europe wild stories spread about America. Crazy, *meshugge*.

Did you ever hear the expression "money doesn't grow on trees"? Well, in our shtetl, we heard in America money *does* grow on trees. So after the trolley ride, when we walked through the crowded streets, we looked hard. No trees. We had also heard, "In America everyone is rich. Money flows like water. Even the streets are paved with gold." Not true! But each block was pretty. One had only shoemakers, another was full of pickle shops, and one was really special. Everywhere were pretty ribbons, pretty hats. I was so hypnotized I bumped smack into Sammy, who was standing stock still staring at all the beautiful signs.

Sammy, who already knew a little English, looked hard at one particular sign. Then he stared at the other signs. He said, "I knew people were rich in America, but who could believe they advertised it?"

We were on the hat maker's street, so the sign said "Milliners." Guess what Sammy thought that meant?

Our Beds

Papa stopped, proudly sweeping off his hat. He bowed deeply. "Welcome to apartment 3A, Twenty-one Ludlow Street, Manhattan, United States of America."

"A family lives here on top of another family, like bees in a hive, sardines in a can? This you call normal?" Tante whined, squinting at the topsy-turvy tenement crammed with railroad flats.

"Come in already. Maybe the flat you'll like better," Papa encouraged as we flew upstairs. He opened the door. Tante pushed past Papa. Her eyes rolled up, her face turned red.

"For this I crossed an ocean?" she groaned, glaring at our railroad flat. A railroad flat, in case you never get invited, is a skinny string of rooms. A window in the front, a window in the back, and good luck in between.

Papa's face fell. Alone he had slaved, starved to save enough to bring his family to America. For us a railroad flat in America was better than any palace in Europe, for here we wouldn't be murdered because we were Jews. Why didn't Tante understand? Instead she bristled about, arranging.

"Itzhak, put down the bags here," she ordered, pointing to the nicest room. "Heike, darling, here's a lovely bed just for you!" For Papa, she also found a corner to hide in. Then Tante pushed together two chairs in the kitchen.

"Gussie, look how special!" she simpered.

That night Papa got rope. He tied the chairs tight, covered me with a feather quilt, kissed me good night, and whispered, "Mama will come soon, my Goldala. Don't worry, you'll see. Dream sweetly."

And I did.

Maybe you wondered, "Where are Sammy and Louie?" The "cockroaches" also get very special beds that got them that special cruel nickname I made up. (I'm ashamed to say.)

"Cockroach, cockroach," I used to tease, running madly from my two tiny older brothers. They were really short. Now I know why. The flat was so crowded my beloved cockroaches had to sleep in the front room. So? So this was Papa's store. Woolen goods piled from top to bottom made soft, warm, good beds. But who knows what breathing fabric fumes all night could do to a young boy's health? Sammy and Louie never complained. In those days nobody thought of such things. But neither Sammy nor Louie ever grew tall like Papa.

School

Miss Daly marched into the classroom.

Quick we jumped to our feet. "Good morning, Miss Daly," we chanted.

"Good morning, students. You may sit," Miss Daly replied.

We sat straight, hands clasped tight behind our backs. We did not look here, we did not look there, we looked only at our teacher. She held up a big sign. Loudly she pronounced, "GOOD HEALTH COMES FROM GOOD FOOD."

"Repeat after me, three times please," she ordered.

Did we have a choice? So three times we repeated, "Good health comes from good food."

"You people are ignorant! The food you eat is not good food," she proclaimed. "Your teeth will rot, your bones will break, you'll sicken and die if you continue to eat that awful, fatty, starchy, colorless stuff you ate in Europe. It is your duty to be healthy American children, and I will tell you how."

My hair stood on end! Our food was not good? Our food was better than good. It was delicious. Colorless? I fell into a dream. Knishes, knaidlach, potato pancakes with fried onions. Their color was tan, but, yum, how my mouth watered.

Miss Daly unrolled a huge poster.

"Augusta Schmukler, stand up. What is this?" Miss Daly asked.

I shook. "I don't know, Miss Daly."

"This is broccoli," she said.

"What is broccoli?" I asked.

Do you know how it is to be scared all the time in school?

You don't? Doesn't your teacher carry a big ruler, ready to rap your knuckles, wear clothes from I don't know where? Stiff, high collars, hard-starched shirt fronts, tight, tight hair that makes her eyes pop?

Miss Daly told us about green things and red things and yellow things to eat.

"So, Augusta," she continued, "tell us, do you eat green vegetables at home?"

"Yes, Miss Daly," I stammered.

"And what vegetable is that, may I ask?" she said, looking down her nose.

At last I knew the answer to a question. "A pickle!" I said proudly.

So why did everyone laugh?

The Hurdy-Gurdy

Have you every heard a hurdy-gurdy? Why would you? Today, push a button, you get music! We didn't have such a luxury. We made music. Hopping on one foot we'd sing silly songs.

Tzigelle migelle, ckota na.
Chaim, auf tza luches.
or
Eingeh, beingeh, stupeh, tsaingeh—hop!

Immediately Tante would wrap her head in a rag, moaning, "Quiet, shaa. Oooh, mein head!"

She had one of her famous headaches. What's a headache? An ache is a pain. A pain comes from a kick, a slap, a smack. But who would dare hit Tante over the head, no matter how much he wanted to? So we couldn't sing much. Mostly our music came from the hurdy-gurdy man. Such a treat!

His music made me whirl and twirl till the hurdy-gurdy man's little monkey shook the cup for people's pennies. I never had a penny, but my friend Lena put one in. Monkey bowed. Sadly we watched them walk away. Until one day we couldn't stop dancing. We held hands. We followed the music, following, following, dancing, dancing. Following the hurdy-gurdy man.

Suddenly it was dark. How could this happen? We blinked back tears. Where were we? Dirty water. Filthy docks. No more hurdy-gurdy man. Oy, we were lost. Lena cried. I saw a fire station. Firemen—them we knew; they were always kind. We barely spoke English, but the firemen figured we were lost. One friendly fellow made magic. He blinked, he winked; from my ear came two peppermints. One for me, one for Lena. We forgot to cry! We almost laughed a little. He held our hands, took us here, took us there, until at last we came to Ludlow Street. Lena's mama was running up and down, looking, looking, screaming, "Lena! Lena!" She cried, hugging and kissing Lena. She thanked the good fireman again and again.

When I opened my apartment door, Tante Fanny yelled, "Where were you, you dumbhead. Peel those potatoes before I peel you!" Heike sat chewing chopped liver spread on pumpernickel. She stuck out her greasy tongue and did shame, shame with her fingers.

How I missed my own sweet mama.

So what were the silly songs about? *Tzigella migelle* means something like "To spite Chaim, when Papa hits Mama, all the children dance." Pretty strange, no? *Eingeh beingeh* is even sillier. Only a few words come back. *Stupeh*—stick, *tsaingeh*—finger or maybe tongue. *Beigeleh*—bagel, who knows? It didn't make sense.

No wonder Tante got a headache.

A Place Like the Country

In the old country people walked. Here they raced. People filled the tenements and spilled onto the streets. Pushcarts, wagons pulled by horses, streetcars, and even an occasional automobile jammed the gutters to overflowing. You can imagine there was trash: garbage-piled corners. Every bit of space was put to use to make a living in the Lower East Side of New York City.

In Russia, even in the shtetl there were growing things, green and pretty. But here? Trees? Flowers? Too bad. For them there was no room. Besides, who had time to smell the flowers? Most parents couldn't pay attention to their children even! Grownups were busy, busy, all the time, busy working.

Children worked hard, too. Sammy and Louie got to help Papa, after school of course. Papa showed them how to measure and even how to cut the woolens with his big scissors. They had his attention! Tante paid attention to me. She made sure I did chores before and after school.

But chores were not for Heike. No work for her.

"So delicate, mein Heikala," breathed Tante. "Darling, sit, rest, eat a little." So Heike sat.

But Heike suffered terribly. She was like a pail with a hole in it. No matter how much love and attention we poured in, it seemed to leak out. She couldn't get enough. She was never satisfied. Maybe because she missed Bubba, she missed Zaida,

she missed trees. Bubba and Zaida were out of the question, but trees, it was decided, she could see.

Papa agreed that it was so important to cure Heike that Uncle Itzie must take a day off from work. (In those days nobody knew what it was to take a vacation.)

The very next day Uncle Itzie helped Heike squeeze her chubby arms into her coat. She wrinkled her nose. She pouted. "Feh, Papa, who needs to walk in this snake pit? Phoo!"

"Patience, Heikala, mein entire *kinder,* a walk is good for everyone. Come, Golda, you'll enjoy too," said Uncle mysteriously, as he led us far from Ludlow Street.

Soon the houses didn't lean on one another. Where were all the pushcarts? The crowds had disappeared. This America even smelled different!

We walked and walked until our legs were sore, but with our eyes we drank in such loveliness we felt refreshed. Pretty houses, people dressed like pictures in the library books. No more babushkas. Instead ladies hats had ribbons and feathers. Not a yarmulke or cap in sight. Men wore derbies, fedoras. I even saw a top hat! A true pleasure. Then, miracle of miracles— a place like the country—fields, trees, flowers even. Could you believe? We sat on a bench. We smelled the fresh air and heard birds singing. A park in New York City . . . Heike smiled.

Bedbugs

Itchy, bitey bedbugs lived in everybody's mattress, no matter how clean a person was. So everyone made war on bedbugs. Here's how we did it.

Every Monday when the sun went down, Tante handed me a lighted candle and a pot full of kerosene.

"Gussie, go under the bed and don't come out till you kill all the bedbugs," she said.

If I held the candle too high the bed could burn; if I held it too low I couldn't see. When I caught a bug I had to drop it into the pot. If a spark dropped with it into the kerosene—*va voooom*; good-bye, Charlie! It was a war, disgusting and dangerous, the Bedbug War.

The soldier in our family, like most soldiers in the bedbug war, was the person who could most easily crawl under the bed. The littlest child. Me. So is it a surprise that accidents happened?

Whole tenements burned down, people were hurt, some even died, just because of bed bugs.

I almost lost my life. Only incidentally because of bedbugs. Fires, I told you, we saw very often. Firefighters spraying water, firemen waiting with big canvas hoops to catch people flying from burning windows—that was a common sight.

My biggest fear was fire, but I believed in firemen. So when one day Tante opened the oven door and orange flames shot out (the goose fat caught fire), I knew just what to do. I shot out the kitchen window headfirst, yelling "Fire!" I imagined wherever there was a fire, firemen stood, ready and waiting. I was sure I'd land right in the middle of their canvas hoop, the safety net. Sammy and Louie, sitting by the window having a snack, knew better. They each grabbed an ankle as I zoomed by. Thanks again, my dear brothers.

The Shvitz

Grownups didn't bathe in the kitchen sink. But every week in summer, once a month in winter, I had to pump cold water into a kettle, heat it on the stove, and dump it in the sink. Then the kids plunged in. Not together. One by one. Of course, Tante said, "Heike will be first!" Then me. I was smallest, so maybe I had the littlest dirt. Next came Sammy, who was at least neat. Last, poor sloppy Louie shivered in leftover gray, cold water.

So how did grownups get clean? They went to the shvitz. What is a shvitz? Besides a funny word? Shvitz means sweat. So?

So, picture an ordinary house—you couldn't tell it from any other on the street. Buy a ticket. Peep in. Inside it's a giant bathroom. People running first quick to a shower—oy, it's cold—jumping into the pool, what a luxury. Next and best of all came the shvitz. Look in if you can. See past the clouds of steam gushing from pipes lining a small hot room. See people lie on benches moaning with delight! Why? Torrents of sweat melted trouble, poured off bodies, washing worries away. Then, for a few pennies more, a massage. Everyone got a final treat, a snooze in an airy room, stretched out on a clean sheet on a clean cot. A *machiyah*. A blessing.

Of course, at the shvitz, it was one day men only; only ladies another. This was Tante's dream day, my nightmare. As soon as the men went to work, Tante set a big pot of sweetbreads, chicken, onions, brisket, and potatoes to cook on the stove. Then she dressed carefully, pinched her cheeks, smiled into her mirror, snapped her purse shut, and proclaimed, "Not a dot after

five, Gussie—remember! Heikala, my angel, next time we'll go together to the shvitz."

Out she went, prancing to the shvitz to meet her friends to bathe, sweat, talk, and doze. Guess what I had to do? Through heat, rain, snow, or sleet, I carried that dinner straight out in front of me. I zigzagged around carts speeding down busy streets, scurried past garbage heaped in scary, empty lots to where Tante lay, cozy and comfortable, and pretending to be so sweet. The big hot pot steamed; sweat poured off me—even in winter. I couldn't see my feet or where I was going. My arms ached, my heart pounded. I was terrified I'd slip and spill Tante's precious dinner. Imagine!

When Tante saw the dinner her eyes glistened; in the corner of her mouth stood a spot of spit. Then Tante, at the shvitz, became another person. Who could recognize her? So generous, so kind—to her friends. She smiled.

"Goldala, at last. On the little stove, put down the pot already."

Plates appeared.

"Serve a *bissel* to Mrs. Rothstein. Mrs. Levy, have a taste. There's plenty! Plenty!"

"Golda, how could you be hungry? You ate already, I'm sure, so take back the pot. Don't forget, scrub it good. Remember, tell Heikala the ladies are dying to see her, so next time it's definite I'll bring her. Now, go. Go!"

Someday, Mama and I would go together to the shvitz. I tried to hope.

I Wanted the Streetcar to Kill Me

Every day Tante Fanny sent me shopping. When I got home she always hated everything I bought. I had to take back the eggs with a crack, the skinny chicken, the piece of meat with gristle. Mostly the merchants shrugged their shoulders and just said, "Oy!" But not scary Mr. Berez.

So one day Tante Fanny sniffed the tomato herring I bought. "Return this immediately! Some nerve—he calls this fish fresh?" I wanted to die, to disappear before Mr. Berez's big ears turned red, his fists flew in the air, and he screamed, "You again!"

As the streetcar rumbled toward me, I squeezed my teary eyes shut. I started to cross right in front of it. I prayed that the streetcar would end my miserable life. But at the last second I changed my mind. Too late! BUMP!! Ooooh. My legs flew up, my bottom slid down. Was I dead? Well, not exactly. Fearfully I looked around. Horses, carts, and carriage wheels whizzed by.

This, I knew, wasn't Heaven. This was the edge of the cowcatcher. No? I don't think you ever saw one. In front of the streetcar was placed a giant metal scoop. If a cow happened to wander in front of the streetcar, it shouldn't get hurt. It could fall onto the scoop and be gently wafted along. The cowcatcher didn't know me from a cow, so it scooped me up instead!

Off we went until Mr. Levy, my father's customer, noticed me speeding down the street. He ran, pointing and yelling. "Stop!" The conductor jerked the streetcar to a halt, yanked me out of the cowcatcher, and scolded, "Don't ever pull a prank like that again, young lady!"

He gave me a shake. All the passengers stared.

Oy! I still held that tomato herring straight out in front of me. Now I felt embarrassed to death . . . but lucky for me it isn't that easy to die.

We Moved Up in the World

This story isn't pleasant, but it does have a happy ending.

Nowadays, you don't think twice about going to the bathroom, but back then, it was another story entirely. Outside, behind our building, stood a few little shacks—the privies. We went down the stairs, through the gloomy alley, across the lonely back yard to a little wooden shack. Inside was a wooden bench with a big round hole carved into it. That was our toilet. So, I tried to go as little as humanly possible, and always before sunset.

One evening I got very busy, with what I don't know. I forgot to go to the bathroom. That night, my stomach woke me. Ugh. I couldn't wait. Everyone was sleeping. I tiptoed carefully—*sshhh*. If a mouse sneezed, Sammy heard. The door clicked behind me. I ran down the stairs, across the icy cold yard, knocked on the privy door, lifted the latch, and walked in. I sat gazing at the newspapers we used for toilet paper, if you please, that hung inside the door when I heard *squeeeek!* Someone was outside, trying to get in. Surprised, I said, "It's taken!" The person seemed not to hear. My candle sputtered. Someone was opening the door. Squirming and embarrassed, I hollered, "I said it's taken!" But the door didn't close. A horrible face grinned in at me. "Go away," I screamed. A puffy finger reached to touch my face. Fear drenched my body in cold sweat. I shrieked, "Someone help me!" The person smiled a very peculiar smile as he moved closer. I froze in horror. His body blocked the door. I squeezed my eyes shut. My heart raced, my pulse pounded—BAM BAM BAM—so loud it was all I could hear. I never heard the running feet, crunching snow, not even the shouts "Stop! Stop!"

Suddenly the man toppled forward, not smiling anymore. Like a bug, I was squashed. My big brother Sammy had heard my screams. Now Sammy was glued to his back, kicking, punching, yelling. "Golda, get out fast!"

"Ugh! This *shlechter* crushed me."

I squirmed, twisted, crawled; at last I escaped. Still Sammy hung on.

"Run, Golda, run!" he hollered.

I did. So did the man. Tossing Sammy onto the snow, he jumped over the fence, disappearing into the gloom. What a commotion. Neighbors ran out and comforted me. When Papa heard what happened he was stunned. He decided then and there to move. We moved up in the world to a tenement where on every floor there was a toilet, only four families shared! In the kitchen—a bathtub. Best of all, from every room you saw the sky. Windows! Light! Air! Heaven! But one I couldn't enjoy. I was so worried Mama would not learn our new ritzy address and could never find us again.

There Were Castles on Ludlow Street

From the window I was washing I watched the children playing, pretending to be princesses in palaces of ice. Snow crystals sparkled like crowns in their hair as they hollowed crystal caves in the huge snowbanks, then crawled inside to lick icicles melted by flickering candles. A blizzard had buried New York. No school today! Today there were castles on Ludlow Street.

I wanted to play outside too, but Tante barked, "Gussie, clean like you never cleaned before. Everything must shine. Today is special. Chanukah and a special some—" Then, slyly, she stopped speaking!

Heike, licking schmaltz off rye bread, snickered. Heike help? Ha! For a change—Heike had a sniffle.

That morning snow diamonds sealed the windows. Papa opened a bundle.

"Look, Golda, Bubba's menorah. All the way from our old home she sent it. To honor miracles, at sundown we'll light a candle so bright it will rival the moon," he said tenderly, polishing all nine branches of the menorah.

Then gaily he wrapped himself like a present in a big coat, a big hat, and a muffler colored like a rainbow. Huh? No work today? Where was Papa going dressed up like a prince?

Now the house smelled delicious. A million onions I sliced—till my eyes were twin fountains, my nose a waterfall—sizzled in goose fat. A potch here, again a potch, *ppft*. From the tons of potatoes I grated, Tante produced perfect pancakes. No king could eat better. But what would Mama eat today? I worried. Would matchsticks in a potato be her Chanukah lamp?

Could being good make wishes come true? Not so far. My tears mixed with the suds in my pail. I felt so sorry for myself that I didn't notice a happy couple with a bundled baby wildly waving up at me. I didn't notice when quick like lightning they flashed across the street, flew upstairs, and flung open our door. I turned from the window I was washing, rubbing my eyes with soapy fingers. From soap bubbles come visions? I couldn't believe the miracle. Not until Mama held me in her arms, and I held Molly in mine, everybody hugging, laughing, kissing, did my tears stop falling. Sammy, Louie, Papa, Molly, and me, my whole family danced, spinning with joy! Uncle Itzhak, of course, joined in. Even Tante and Heike couldn't resist!

Mama, a queen safe in her castle, whispered, "Believe, Goldala, wishes can come true."

My golden life in the Golden Land truly began, as light and bright as the whole menorah shining.

Glossary

Babushka	An "old grandmother" a scarf worn on a woman's head; a kerchief
Bissel	A little bit
Borsht	Yummy vegetable soup with a beet or cabbage base
Bubba	Grandma
Chanukah	Chanukah is a happy holiday commemorating miracles. In 1065 B.C. a small band of Maccabees triumphed over the enormous armies of tyranny. In the temple they found only enough undefiled oil to burn for one night. It burned for eight! Jews honor this miracle by lighting the menorah. Each night for eight days Jews light the menorah—one candle, then two, then three, until eight candles are lit. The ninth candle is a special candle that is used to light all the others. Songs are sung, presents are given, and games are played.
Farfel	Little drops of noodle dough boiled in salty water and served with gravy
Gott	God
Himmel	Heaven
Hurdy-gurdy	A large, portable, wind-up music box
Ketzalah	Little cat
Kindele	Little children
Kinder	Children
Knish	A delicious patty stuffed with onions and meat or potatoes
Kvetch	To complain
Maidella	Little girl
Mein entire kinder	All my children
Menorah	A nine-branched candleholder (see Chanukah)
Meshugge	Crazy
Pletzle	A crisp cookie
Samovar	A large urn for brewing tea
Schlecter	Bad one
Schmaltz	Rendered fat, usually chicken fat
Shissel	A basin
Shtetl	A small village or ghetto where Jews lived
Shvitz	A communal bath. Ladies and gentlemen were permitted in the baths on alternate days.
Tante	Aunt
Zaida	Grandpa